HEWLETT-WOODMERE PUBLIC LIBRARY
HEWLETT, NEW YORK

D1383882

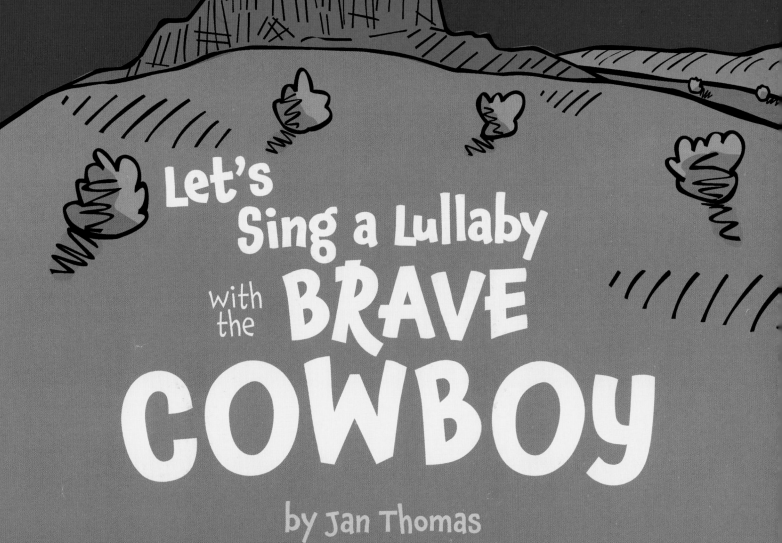

Let's Sing a Lullaby with the BRAVE COWBOY

by Jan Thomas

BEACH LANE BOOKS · New York London Toronto Sydney New Delhi

Is that a HUGE HAIRY SPIDER over there?!!

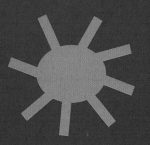

But is there a
LARGE
LUMBERING
BEAR
behind me?!!

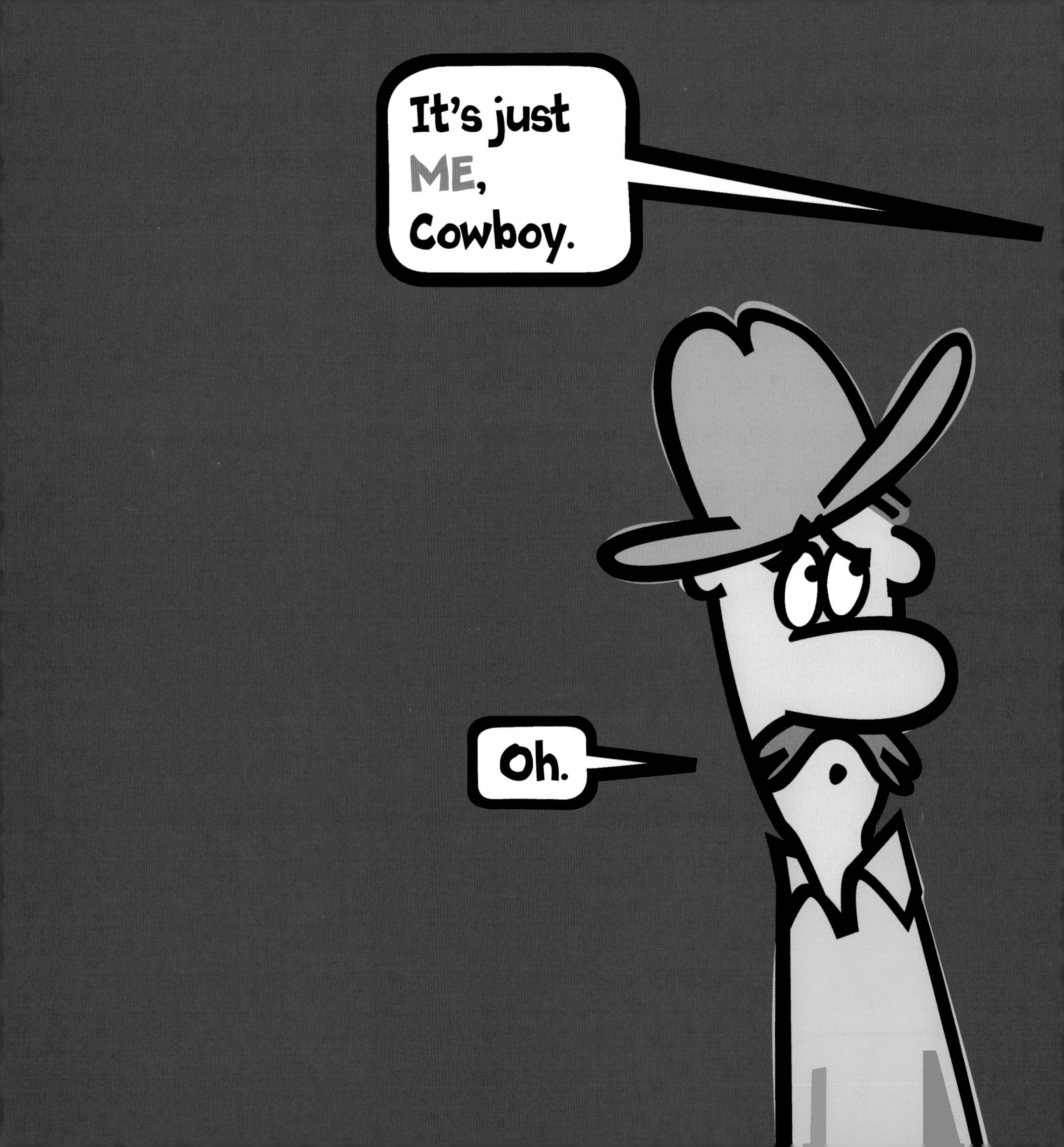
It's just ME, Cowboy.
Oh.

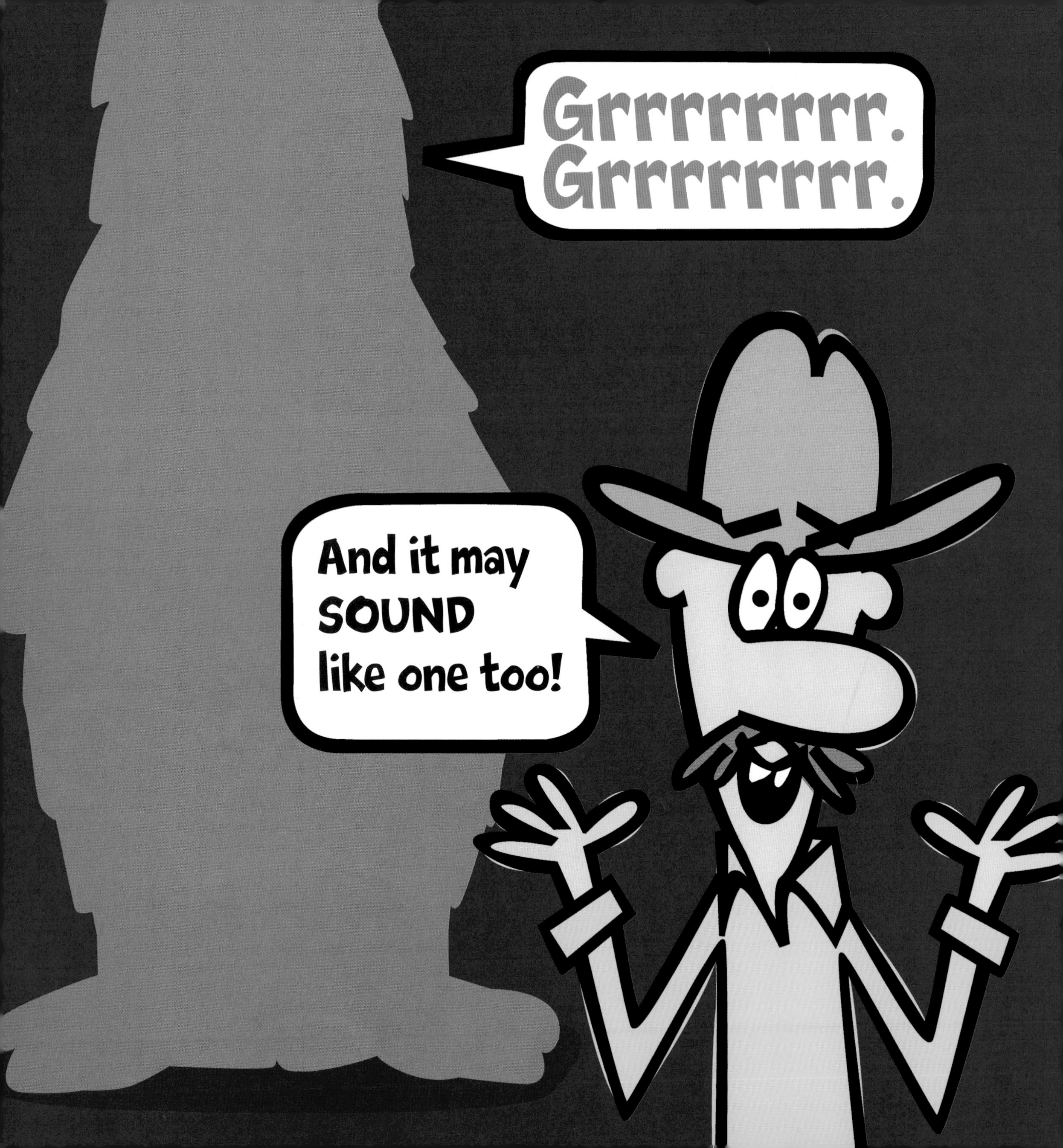
Grrrrrrrr. Grrrrrrrr.
And it may SOUND like one too!

Um, do wolves like lullabies?

APR 24 2013

HEWLETT-WOODMERE PUBLIC LIBRARY

3 1327 00570 8771